GRAPHIC LIBRARY™

HIGH-TECH HIGHWAYS AND SUPER SKYWAYS

THE NEXT 100 YEARS OF TRANSPORTATION

by Nikole Brooks Bethea

CAPSTONE PRESS
a capstone imprint

Graphic Library is published by Capstone Press,
1710 Roe Crest Drive, North Mankato, Minnesota 56003
www.mycapstone.com

Library of Congress Cataloging-in-Publication data is available on the Library of Congress website.
ISBN 978-1-4914-8266-7 (library binding)
ISBN 978-1-4914-8270-4 (eBook PDF)

Editor
Mandy Robbins

Art Director
Nathan Gassman

Designer
Ted Williams

Media Researcher
Jo Miller

Production Specialist
Katy LaVigne

Illustrator
Alan Brown

Colorist
Giovanni Pota

Design Element: Shutterstock: pixelparticle (backgrounds)

Printed and bound in the United States of America.
009679F16

TABLE OF CONTENTS

SECTION ONE WHERE HAVE WE BEEN?

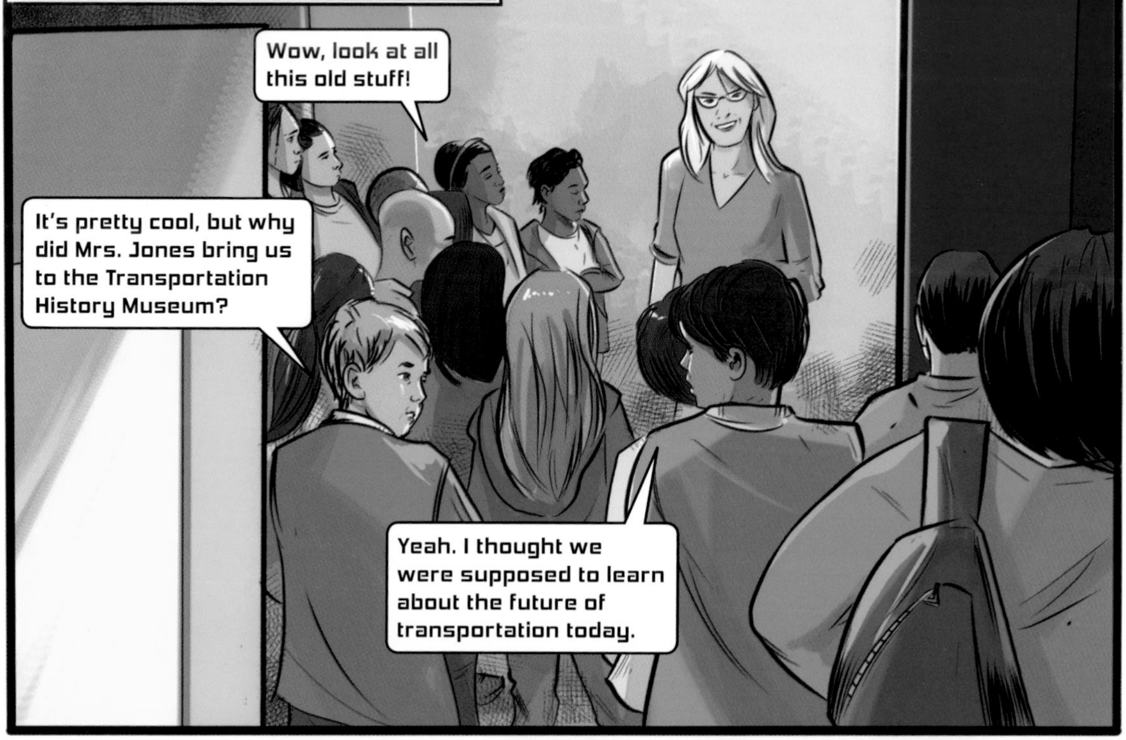
Wow, look at all this old stuff!
It's pretty cool, but why did Mrs. Jones bring us to the Transportation History Museum?
Yeah. I thought we were supposed to learn about the future of transportation today.

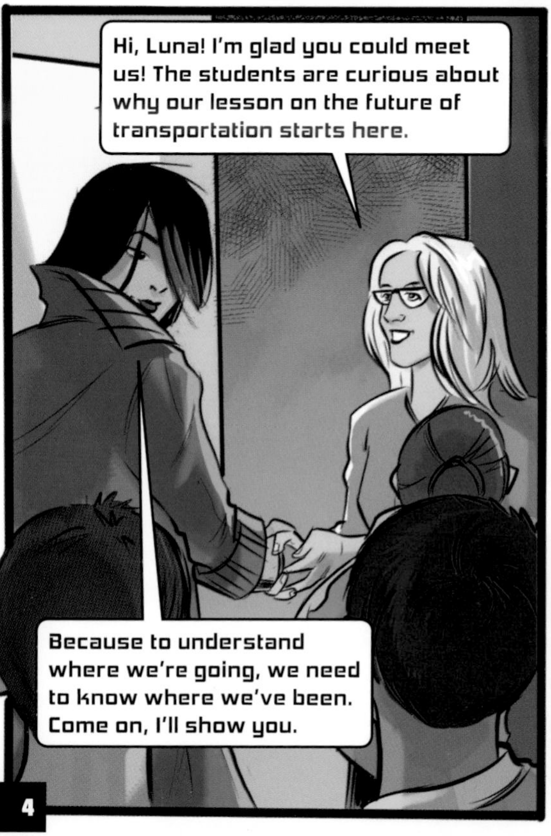
Hi, Luna! I'm glad you could meet us! The students are curious about why our lesson on the future of transportation starts here.
Because to understand where we're going, we need to know where we've been. Come on, I'll show you.

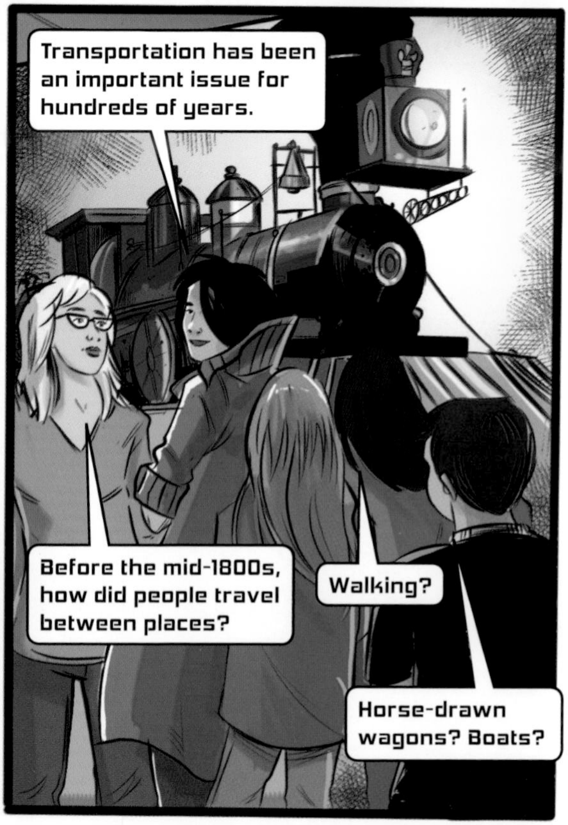
Transportation has been an important issue for hundreds of years.
Before the mid-1800s, how did people travel between places?
Walking?
Horse-drawn wagons? Boats?

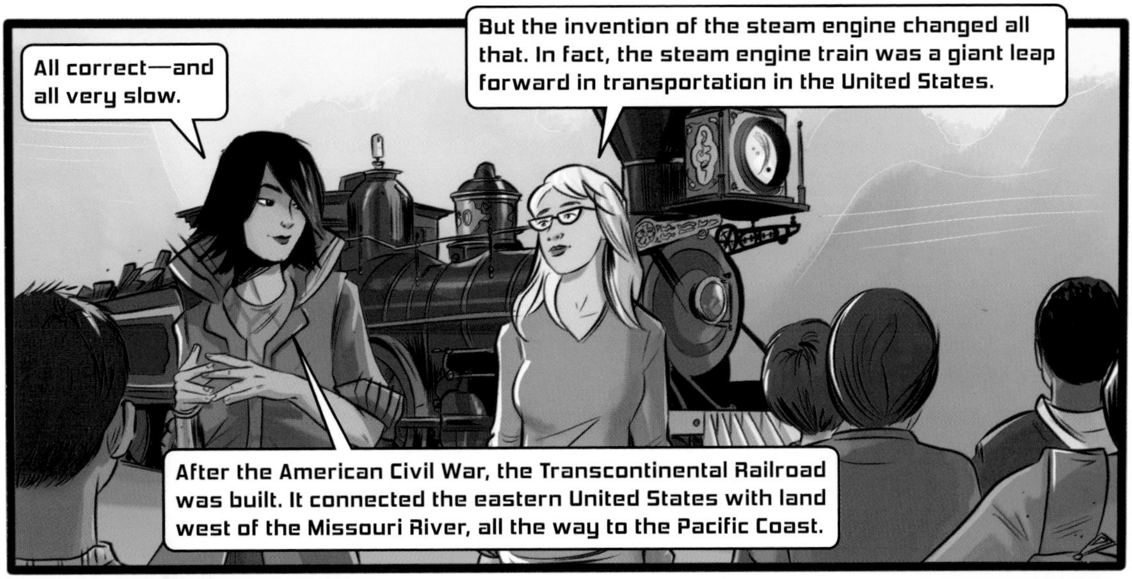
All correct—and all very slow.
But the invention of the steam engine changed all that. In fact, the steam engine train was a giant leap forward in transportation in the United States.
After the American Civil War, the Transcontinental Railroad was built. It connected the eastern United States with land west of the Missouri River, all the way to the Pacific Coast.

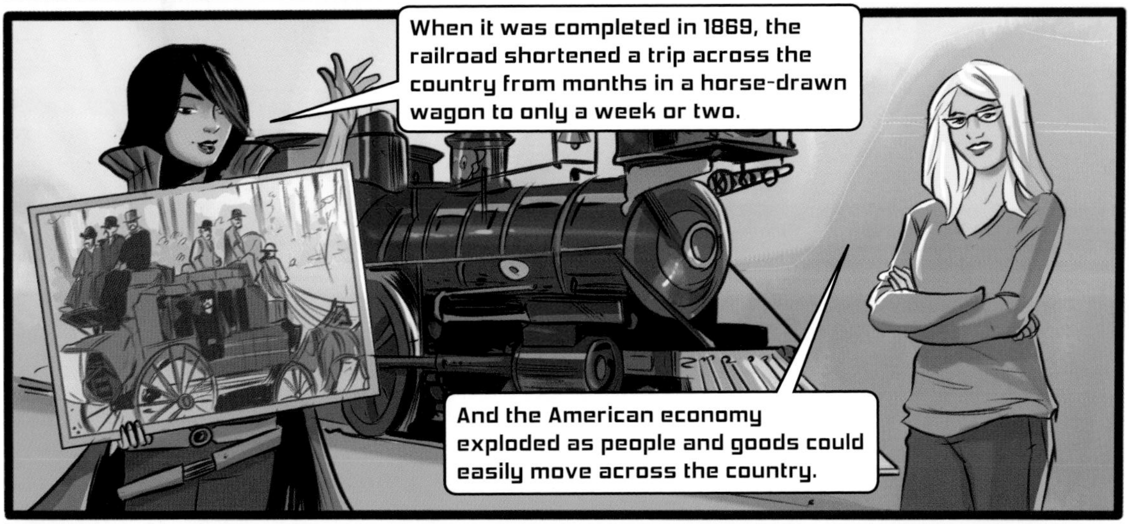
When it was completed in 1869, the railroad shortened a trip across the country from months in a horse-drawn wagon to only a week or two.
And the American economy exploded as people and goods could easily move across the country.

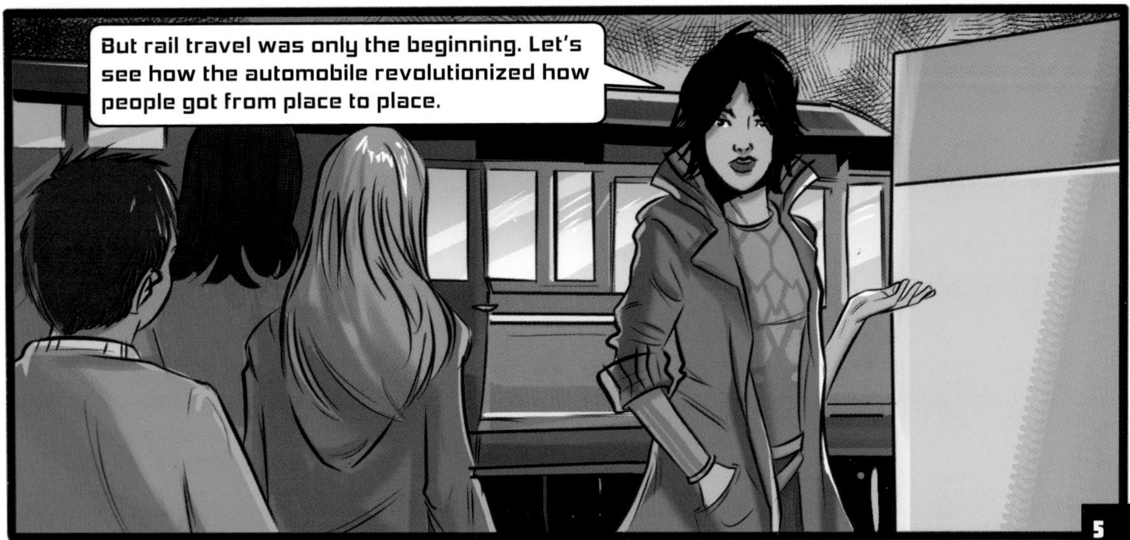
But rail travel was only the beginning. Let's see how the automobile revolutionized how people got from place to place.

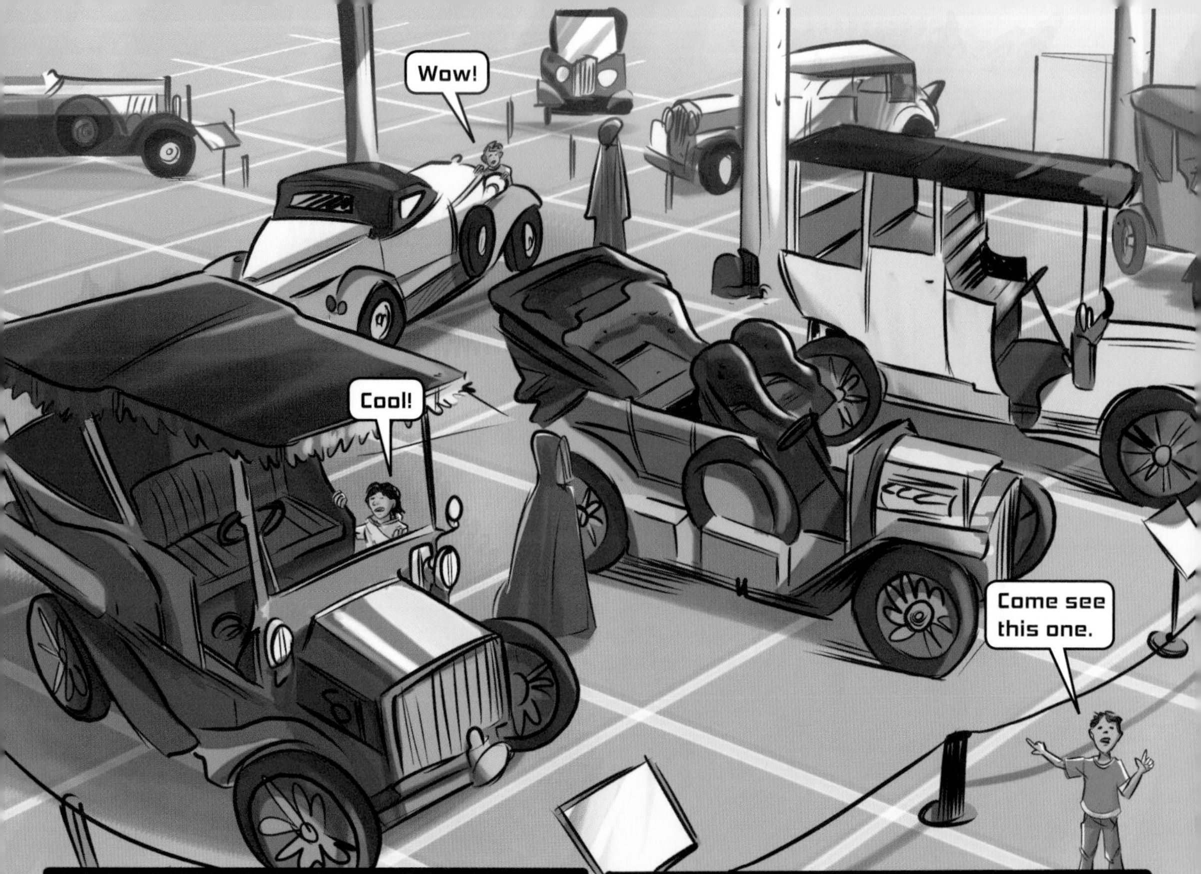
Wow!
Cool!
Come see this one.

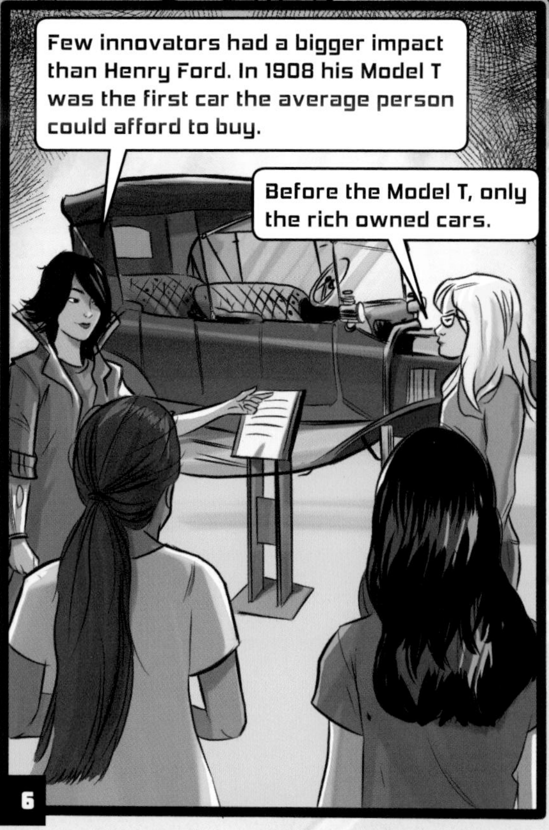
Few innovators had a bigger impact than Henry Ford. In 1908 his Model T was the first car the average person could afford to buy.
Before the Model T, only the rich owned cars.

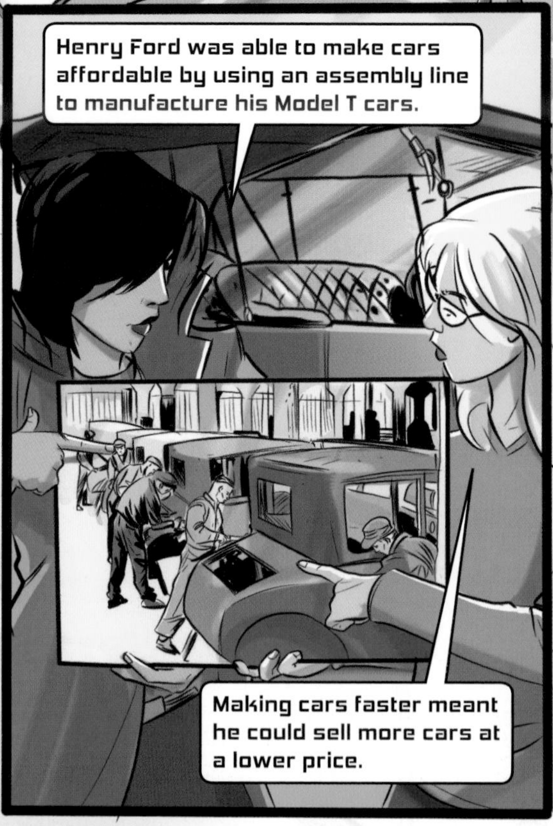
Henry Ford was able to make cars affordable by using an assembly line to manufacture his Model T cars.
Making cars faster meant he could sell more cars at a lower price.

Owning cars let people move out of the cities. They no longer had to live close to railroad stations.

The convenience of automobiles gave people new freedoms. They traveled when and where they wanted.

Cars changed a lot from the Model T Ford to the 1950s and 1960s.

That's nothing compared to cars today. My mom just bought a hybrid. It combines gas and electric power.

We are always improving technology. Cars have gotten faster, safer, and smarter. But to discover even faster travel, let's check out air transportation.

STREETCARS |||||||||||||||

All forms of transportation evolve over time. Consider the streetcar. In 1832 New York's first streetcars were pulled along steel rails by horses. By the 1870s, steam engine-powered cable cars began replacing horse-drawn streetcars. Moving cables between the tracks hauled these people-movers continuously down the streets. In the late 1880s, streetcars powered by electric overhead wires began to replace cable cars. But this technology soon gave way to subways, buses, and other forms of public transportation in the 1900s.

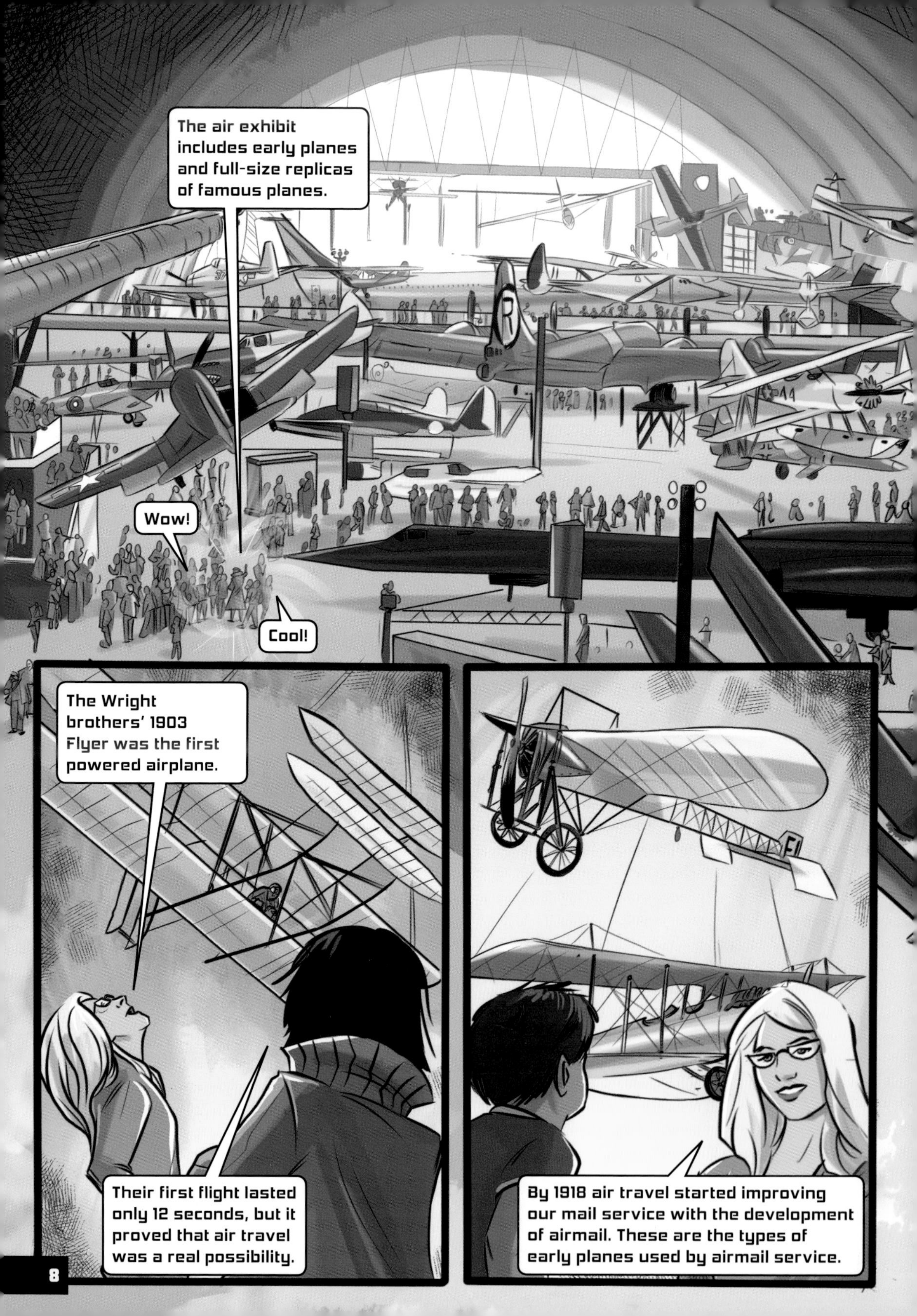
The air exhibit includes early planes and full-size replicas of famous planes.
Wow!
Cool!
The Wright brothers' 1903 Flyer was the first powered airplane.
Their first flight lasted only 12 seconds, but it proved that air travel was a real possibility.
By 1918 air travel started improving our mail service with the development of airmail. These are the types of early planes used by airmail service.

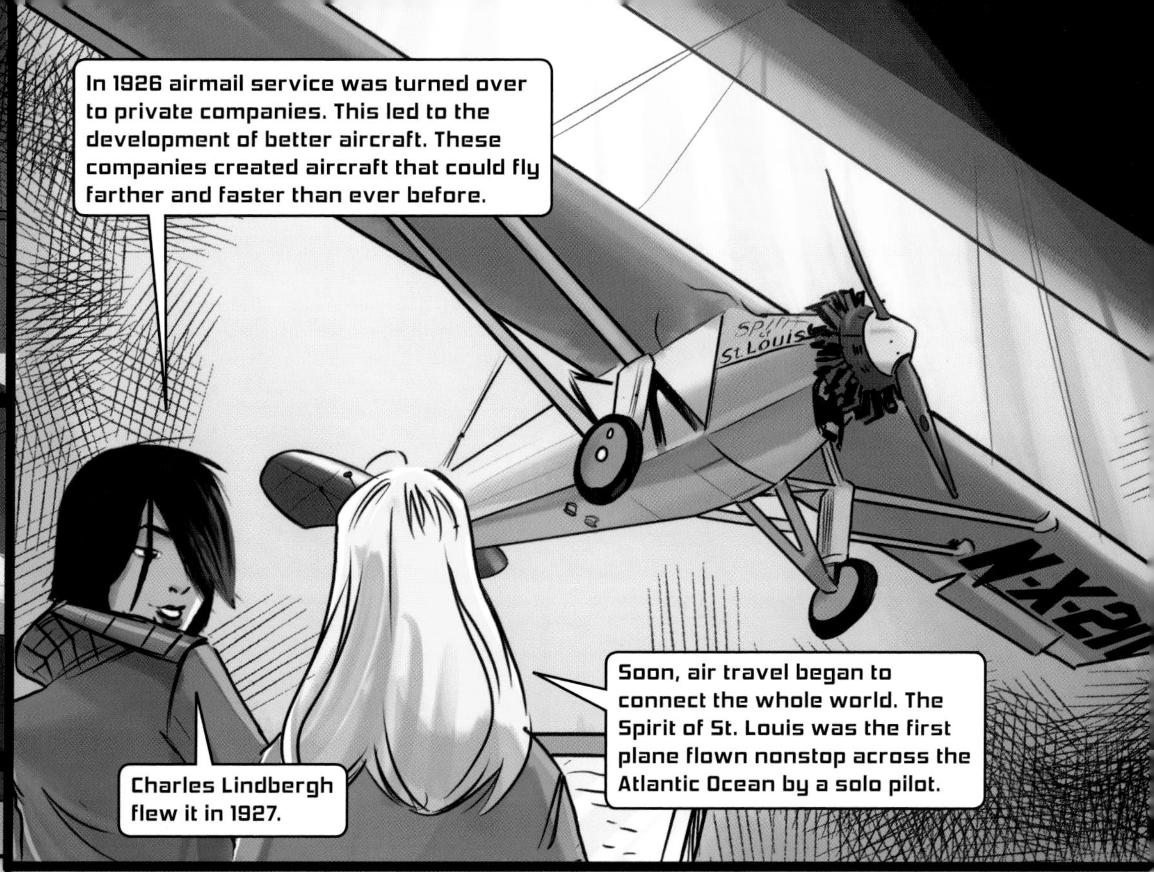
In 1926 airmail service was turned over to private companies. This led to the development of better aircraft. These companies created aircraft that could fly farther and faster than ever before.
Spirit of St. Louis
N-X-211
Soon, air travel began to connect the whole world. The Spirit of St. Louis was the first plane flown nonstop across the Atlantic Ocean by a solo pilot.
Charles Lindbergh flew it in 1927.

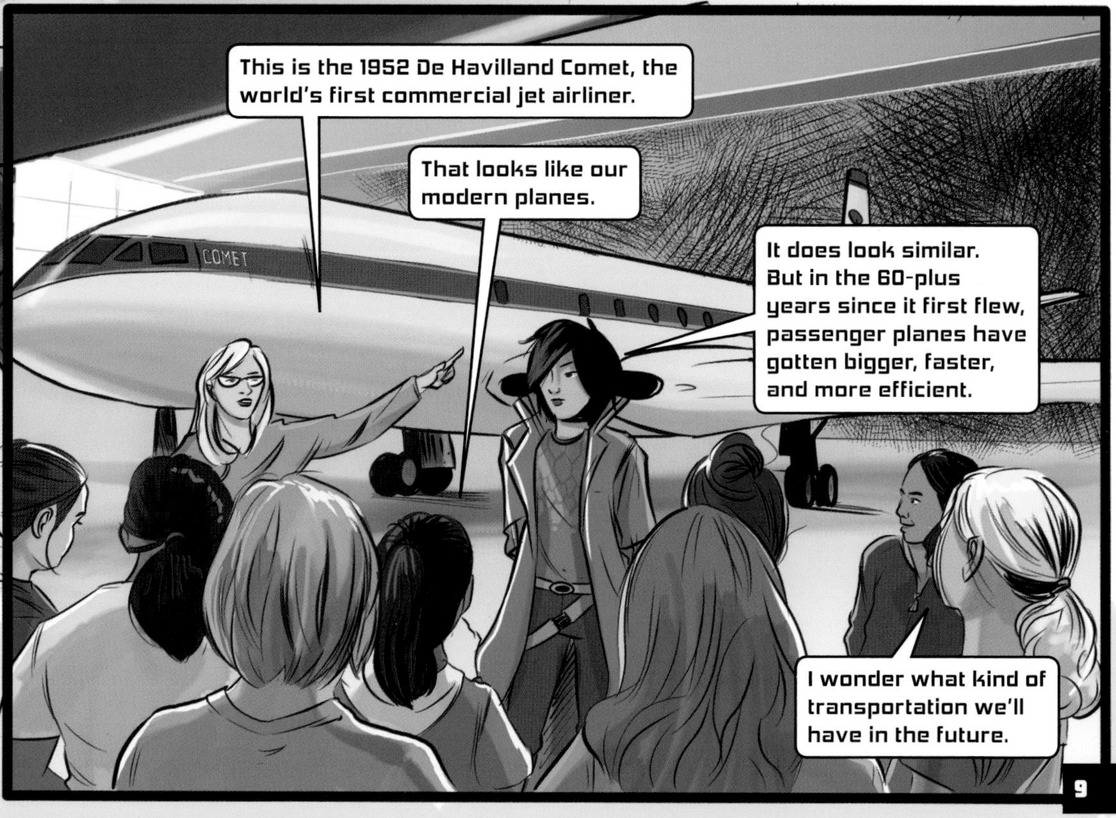
This is the 1952 De Havilland Comet, the world's first commercial jet airliner.
That looks like our modern planes.
COMET
It does look similar. But in the 60-plus years since it first flew, passenger planes have gotten bigger, faster, and more efficient.
I wonder what kind of transportation we'll have in the future.

WHERE ARE WE GOING NEXT?

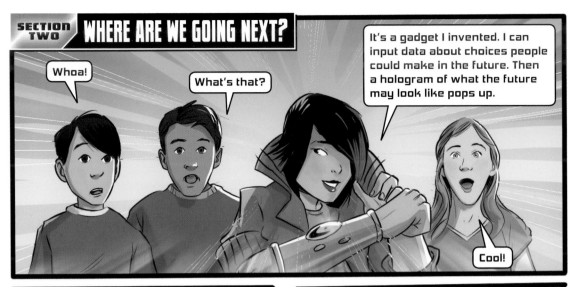

Whoa!

What's that?

It's a gadget I invented. I can input data about choices people could make in the future. Then a hologram of what the future may look like pops up.

Cool!

We know cars are getting smarter and smarter. But will there ever be self-driving cars?

Actually, companies such as Google are already looking into that possibility.

I can't wait to see how self-driving cars might operate.

Excuse me, sir. What did you type in?

My company's address. Now I can eat breakfast and catch up on the daily news on the way to work.

How does the car know where to go?

It uses lasers, radar, and cameras to read road signs and traffic signals.

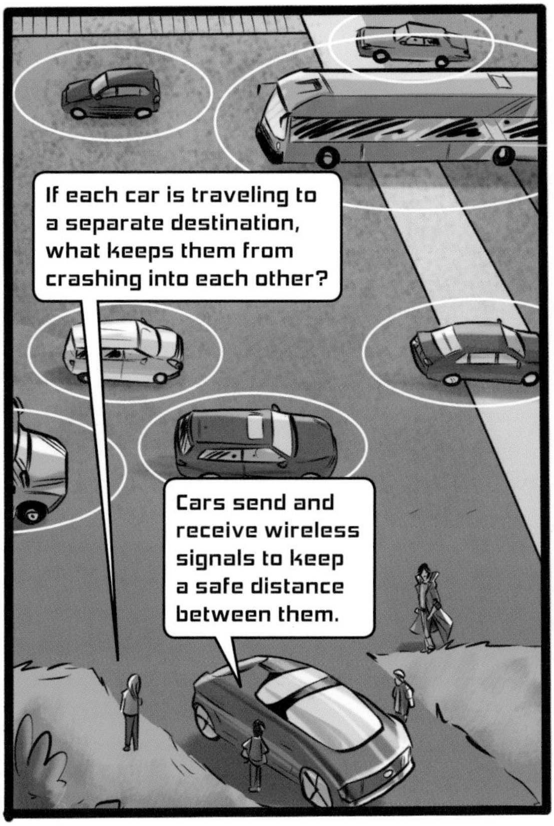
If each car is traveling to a separate destination, what keeps them from crashing into each other?
Cars send and receive wireless signals to keep a safe distance between them.

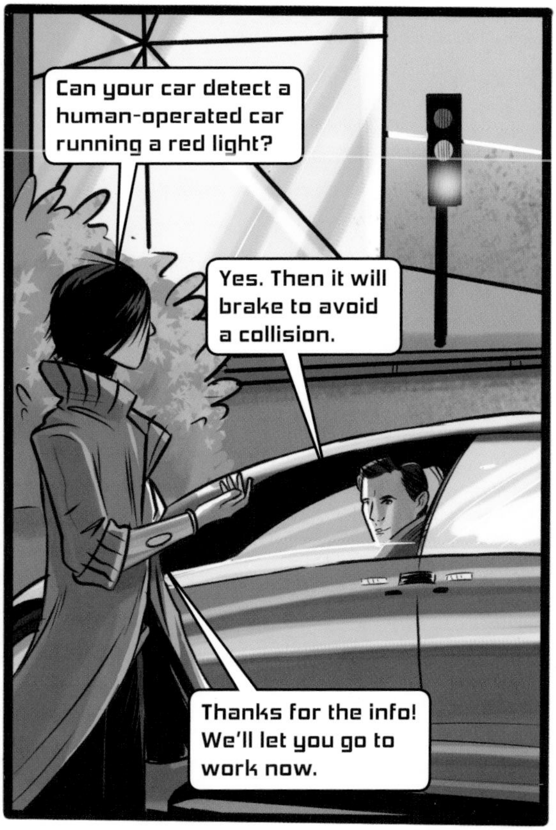
Can your car detect a human-operated car running a red light?
Yes. Then it will brake to avoid a collision.
Thanks for the info! We'll let you go to work now.

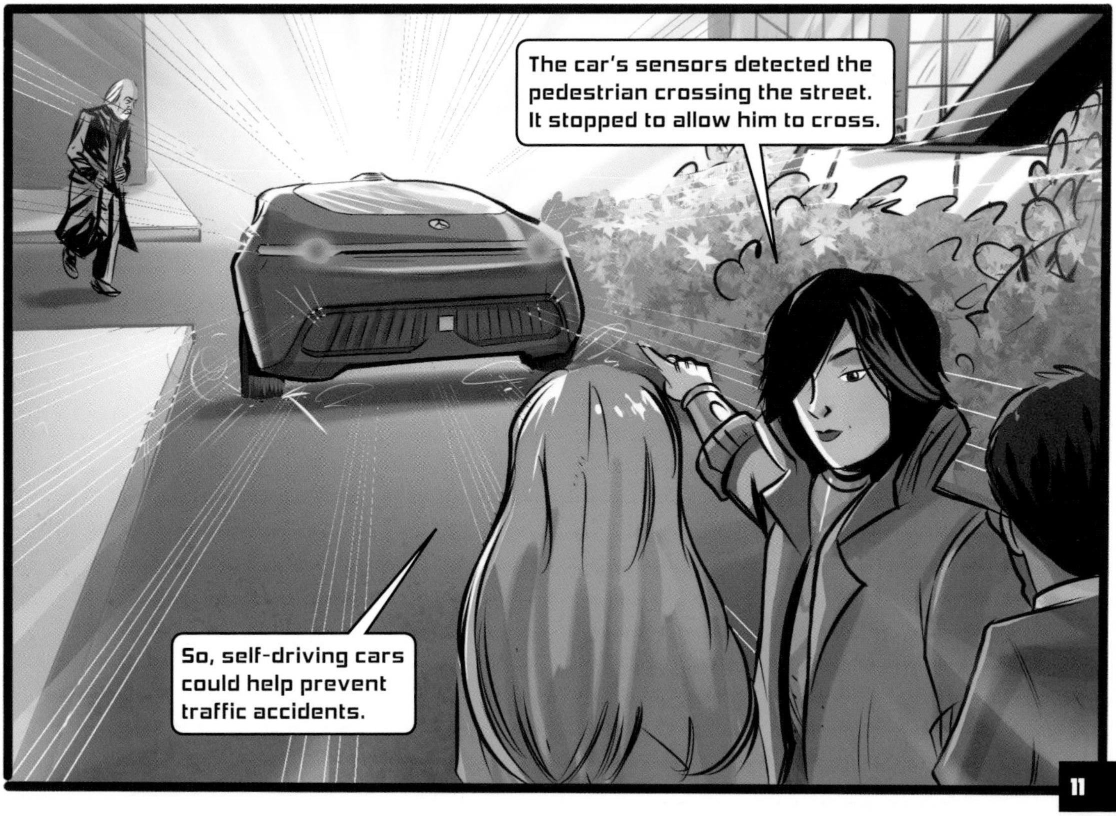
The car's sensors detected the pedestrian crossing the street. It stopped to allow him to cross.
So, self-driving cars could help prevent traffic accidents.

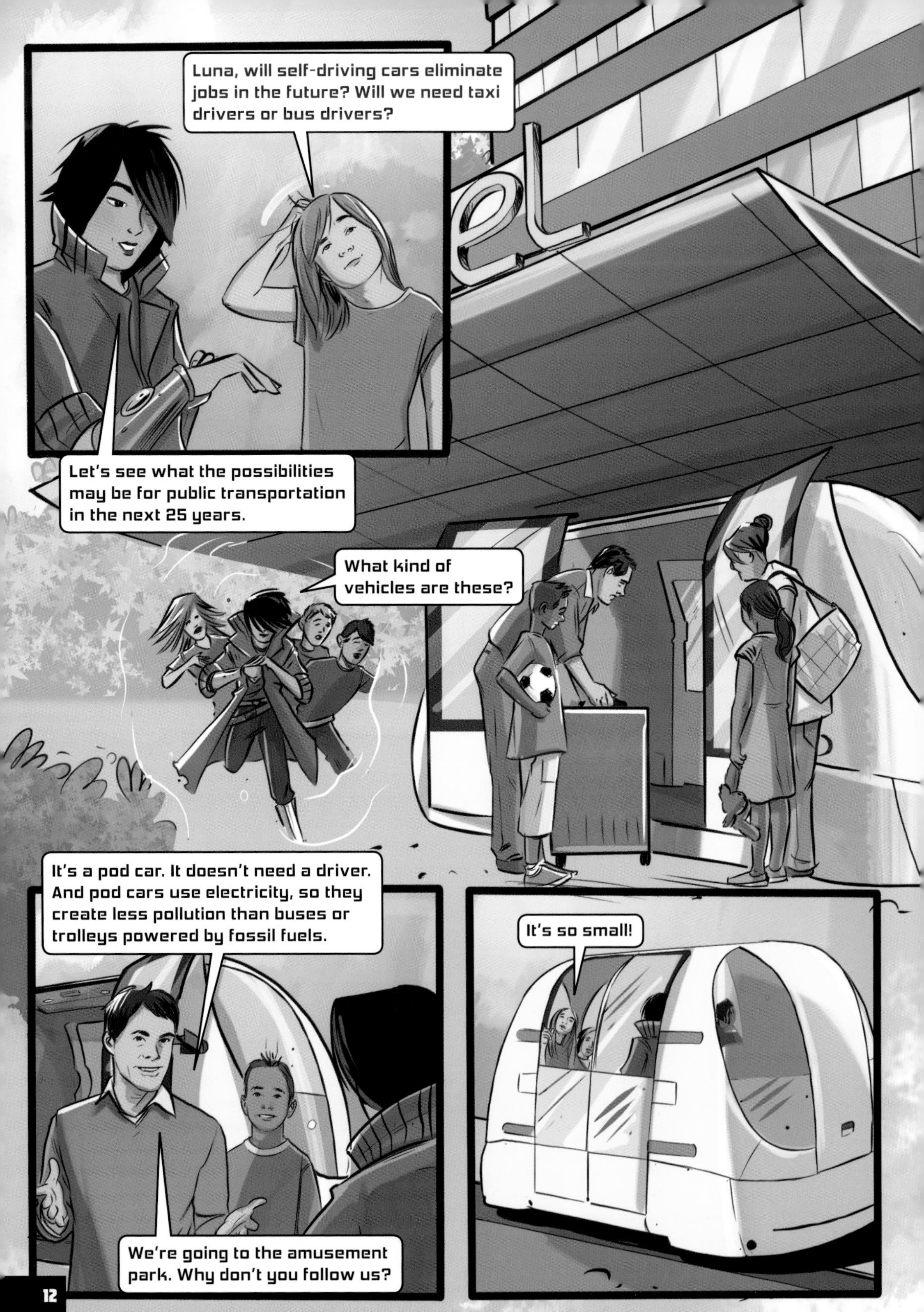
Luna, will self-driving cars eliminate jobs in the future? Will we need taxi drivers or bus drivers?
Let's see what the possibilities may be for public transportation in the next 25 years.
What kind of vehicles are these?
It's a pod car. It doesn't need a driver. And pod cars use electricity, so they create less pollution than buses or trolleys powered by fossil fuels.
We're going to the amusement park. Why don't you follow us?
It's so small!

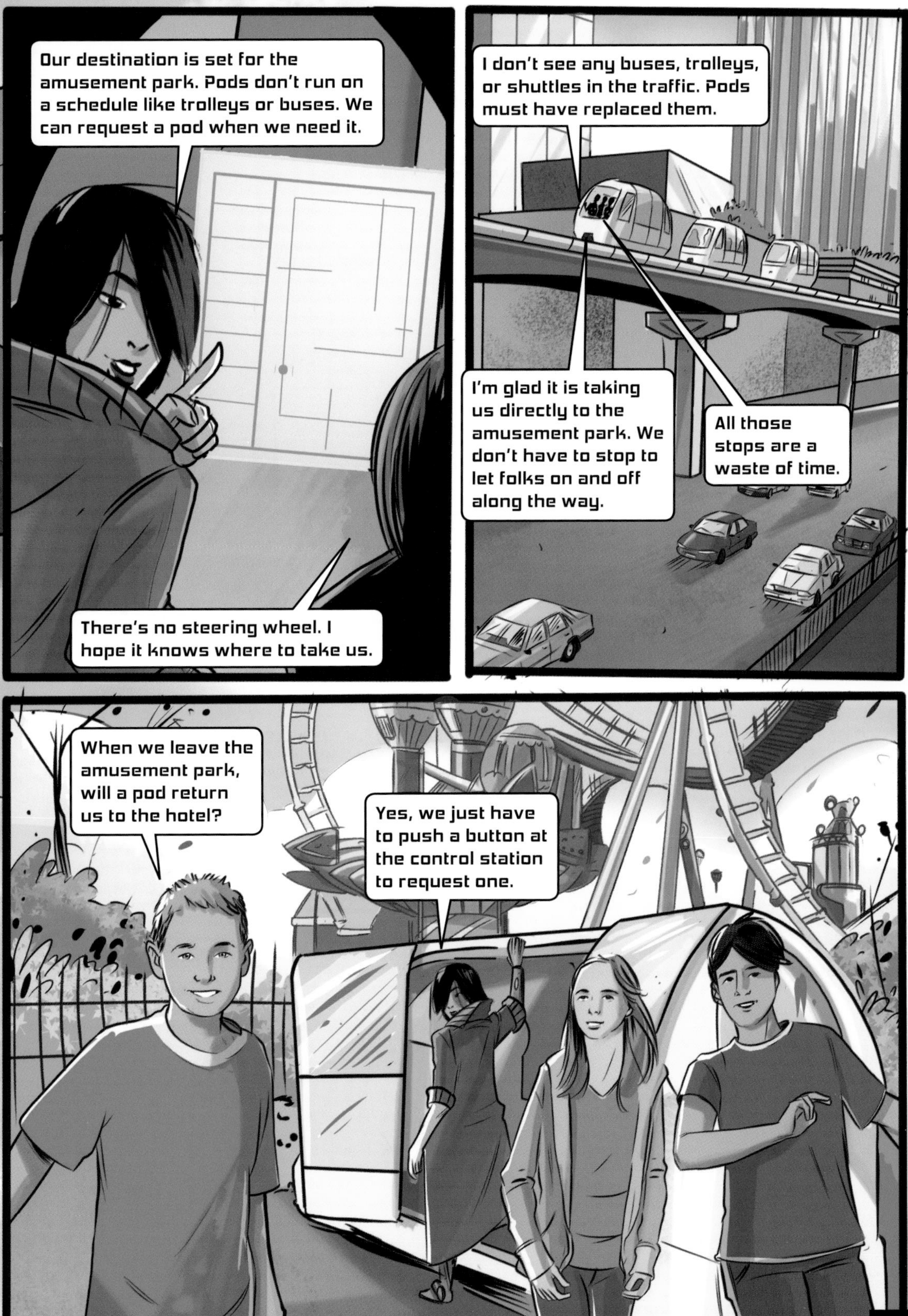
Our destination is set for the amusement park. Pods don't run on a schedule like trolleys or buses. We can request a pod when we need it.
There's no steering wheel. I hope it knows where to take us.
I don't see any buses, trolleys, or shuttles in the traffic. Pods must have replaced them.
I'm glad it is taking us directly to the amusement park. We don't have to stop to let folks on and off along the way.
All those stops are a waste of time.
When we leave the amusement park, will a pod return us to the hotel?
Yes, we just have to push a button at the control station to request one.

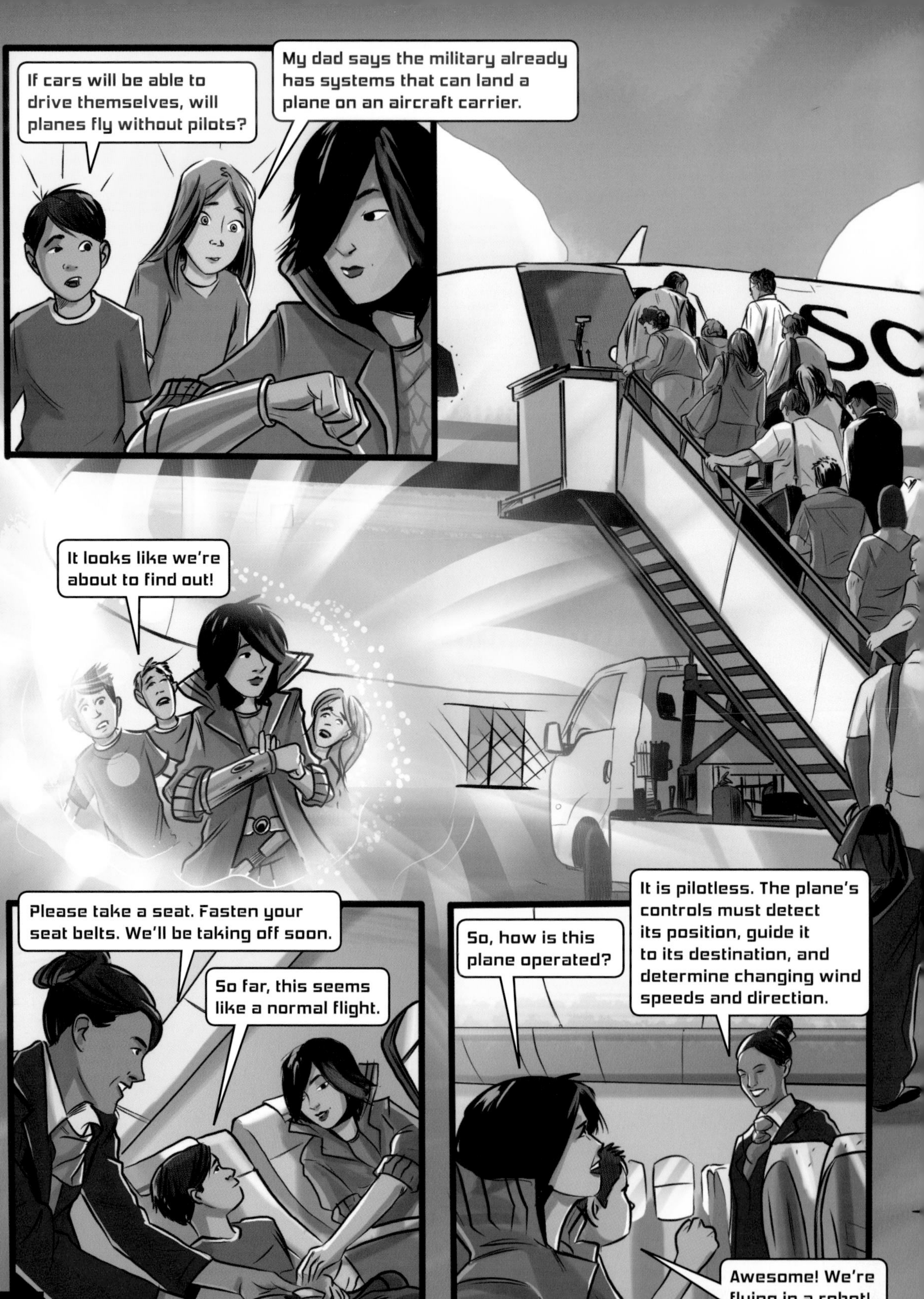
If cars will be able to drive themselves, will planes fly without pilots?
My dad says the military already has systems that can land a plane on an aircraft carrier.
It looks like we're about to find out!
Please take a seat. Fasten your seat belts. We'll be taking off soon.
So far, this seems like a normal flight.
So, how is this plane operated?
It is pilotless. The plane's controls must detect its position, guide it to its destination, and determine changing wind speeds and direction.
Awesome! We're flying in a robot!

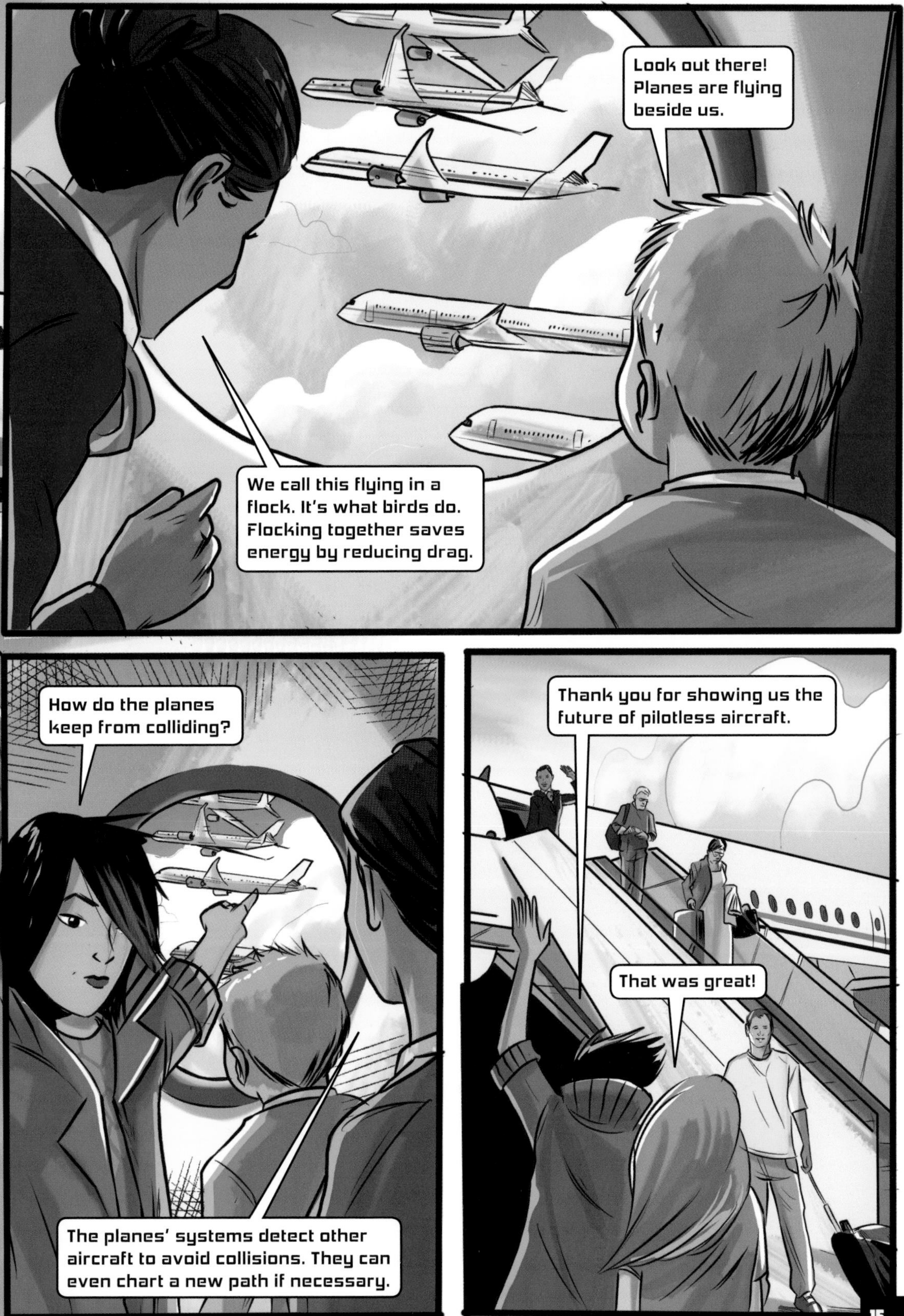
Look out there! Planes are flying beside us.
We call this flying in a flock. It's what birds do. Flocking together saves energy by reducing drag.
How do the planes keep from colliding?
The planes' systems detect other aircraft to avoid collisions. They can even chart a new path if necessary.
Thank you for showing us the future of pilotless aircraft.
That was great!

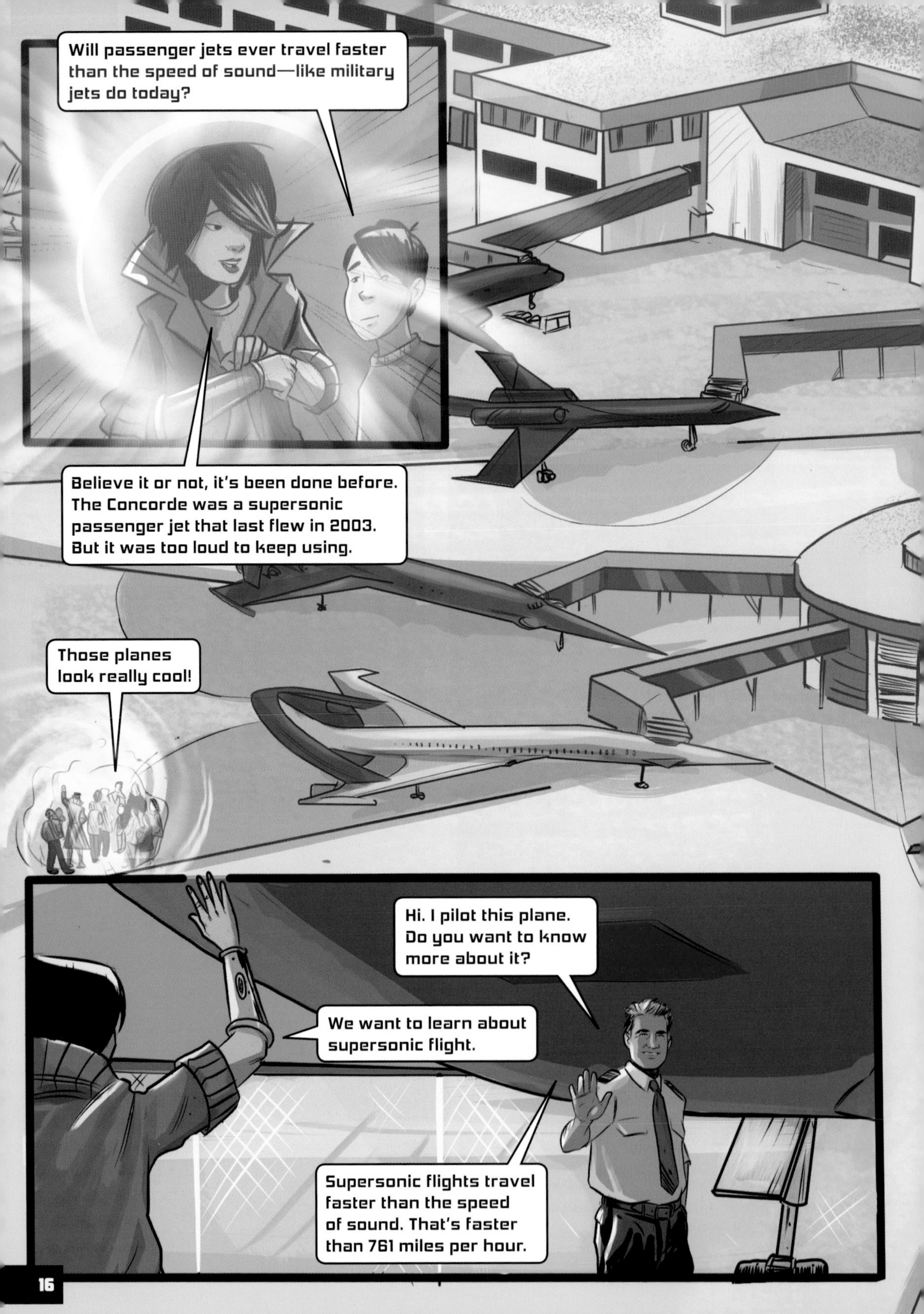
Will passenger jets ever travel faster than the speed of sound—like military jets do today?
Believe it or not, it's been done before. The Concorde was a supersonic passenger jet that last flew in 2003. But it was too loud to keep using.
Those planes look really cool!
Hi. I pilot this plane. Do you want to know more about it?
We want to learn about supersonic flight.
Supersonic flights travel faster than the speed of sound. That's faster than 761 miles per hour.

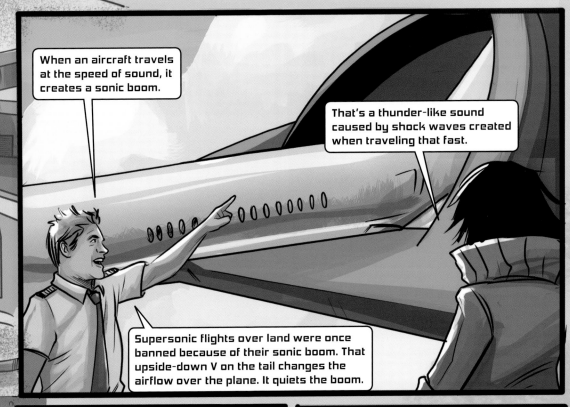

When an aircraft travels at the speed of sound, it creates a sonic boom.

That's a thunder-like sound caused by shock waves created when traveling that fast.

Supersonic flights over land were once banned because of their sonic boom. That upside-down V on the tail changes the airflow over the plane. It quiets the boom.

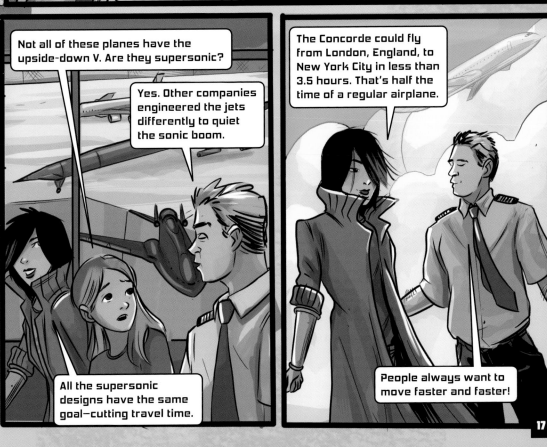

Not all of these planes have the upside-down V. Are they supersonic?

Yes. Other companies engineered the jets differently to quiet the sonic boom.

All the supersonic designs have the same goal—cutting travel time.

The Concorde could fly from London, England, to New York City in less than 3.5 hours. That's half the time of a regular airplane.

People always want to move faster and faster!

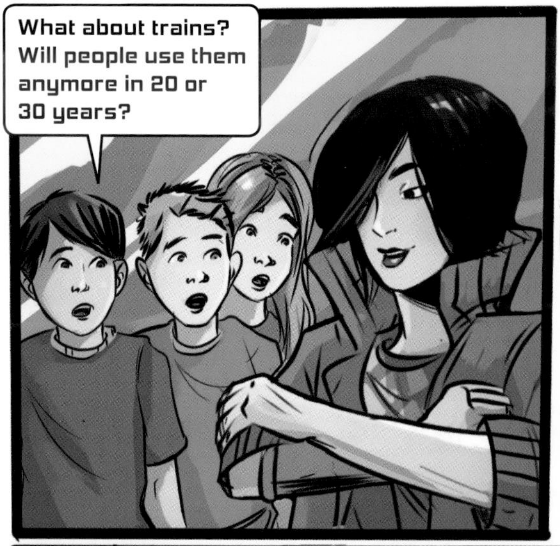
What about trains? Will people use them anymore in 20 or 30 years?

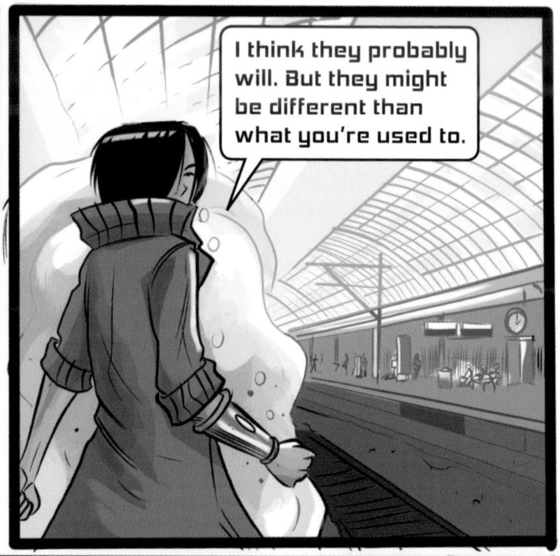
I think they probably will. But they might be different than what you're used to.

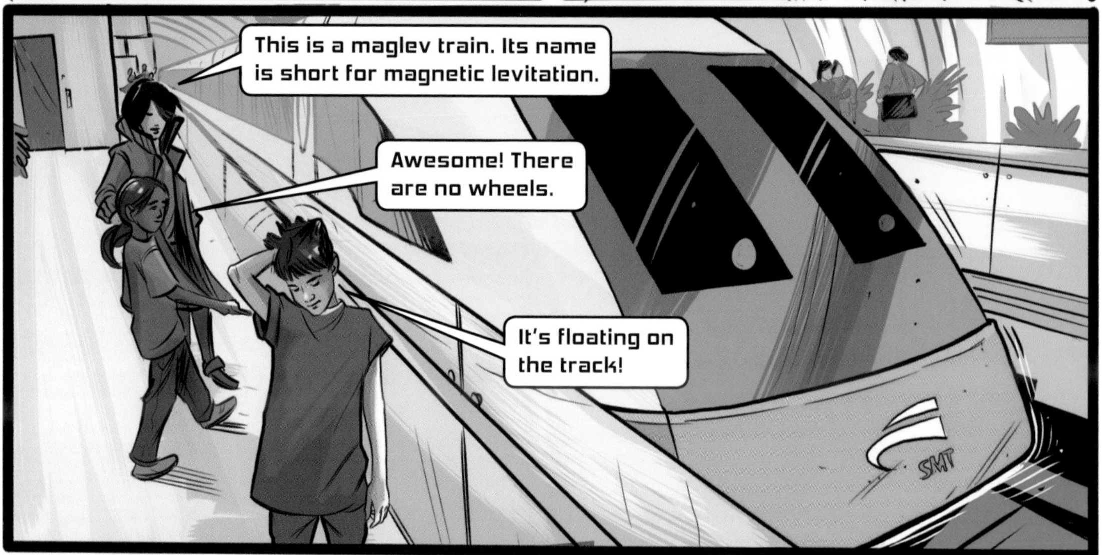
This is a maglev train. Its name is short for magnetic levitation.
Awesome! There are no wheels.
It's floating on the track!
SMT

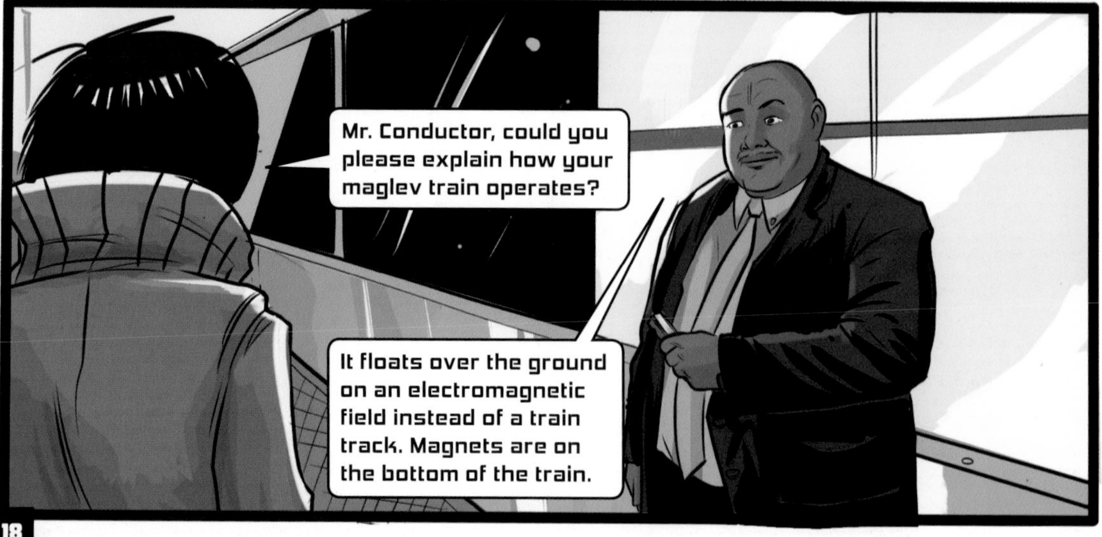
Mr. Conductor, could you please explain how your maglev train operates?
It floats over the ground on an electromagnetic field instead of a train track. Magnets are on the bottom of the train.

HYPERLOOP ||||||||||||||

The Hyperloop is a proposed high-speed transportation system in California. Capsules may one day transport passengers through a large tube from Los Angeles to San Francisco. The 350-mile (563-kilometer) trip is predicted to take about half an hour. The capsules would travel on a cushion of air through the tube at 760 miles (1,223 km) per hour.

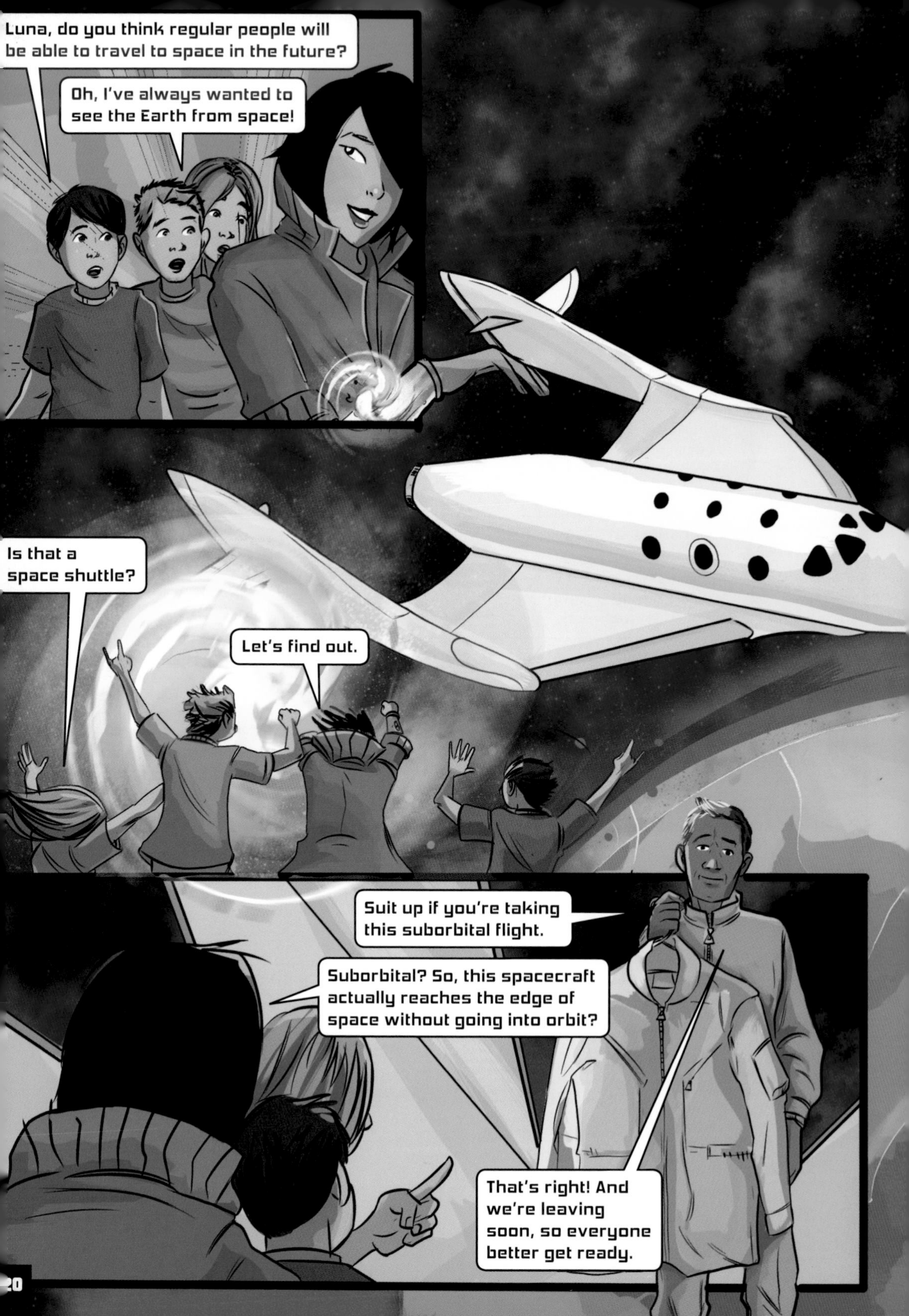
Luna, do you think regular people will be able to travel to space in the future?
Oh, I've always wanted to see the Earth from space!
Is that a space shuttle?
Let's find out.
Suit up if you're taking this suborbital flight.
Suborbital? So, this spacecraft actually reaches the edge of space without going into orbit?
That's right! And we're leaving soon, so everyone better get ready.

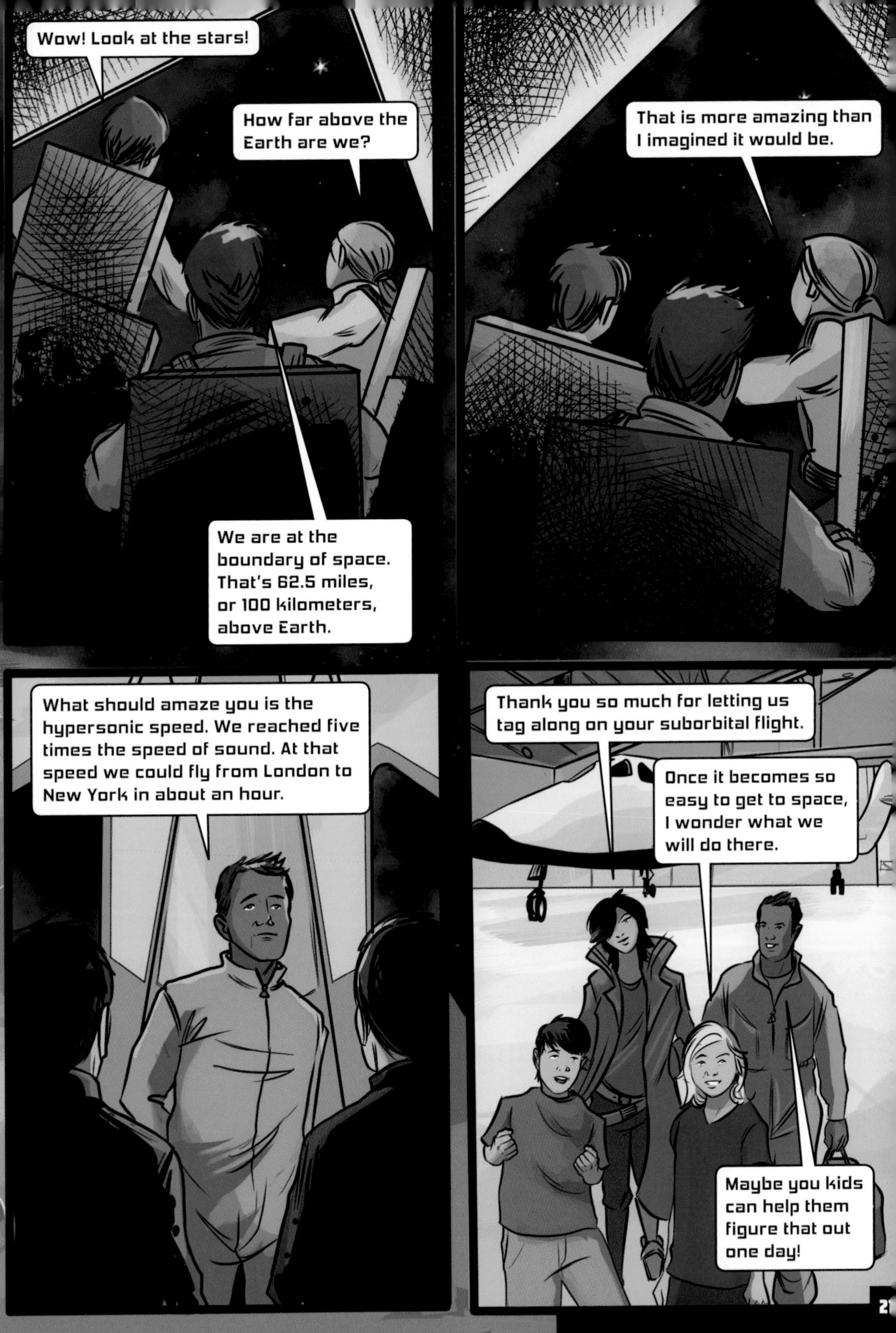
Wow! Look at the stars!
How far above the Earth are we?
We are at the boundary of space. That's 62.5 miles, or 100 kilometers, above Earth.
That is more amazing than I imagined it would be.
What should amaze you is the hypersonic speed. We reached five times the speed of sound. At that speed we could fly from London to New York in about an hour.
Thank you so much for letting us tag along on your suborbital flight.
Once it becomes so easy to get to space, I wonder what we will do there.
Maybe you kids can help them figure that out one day!

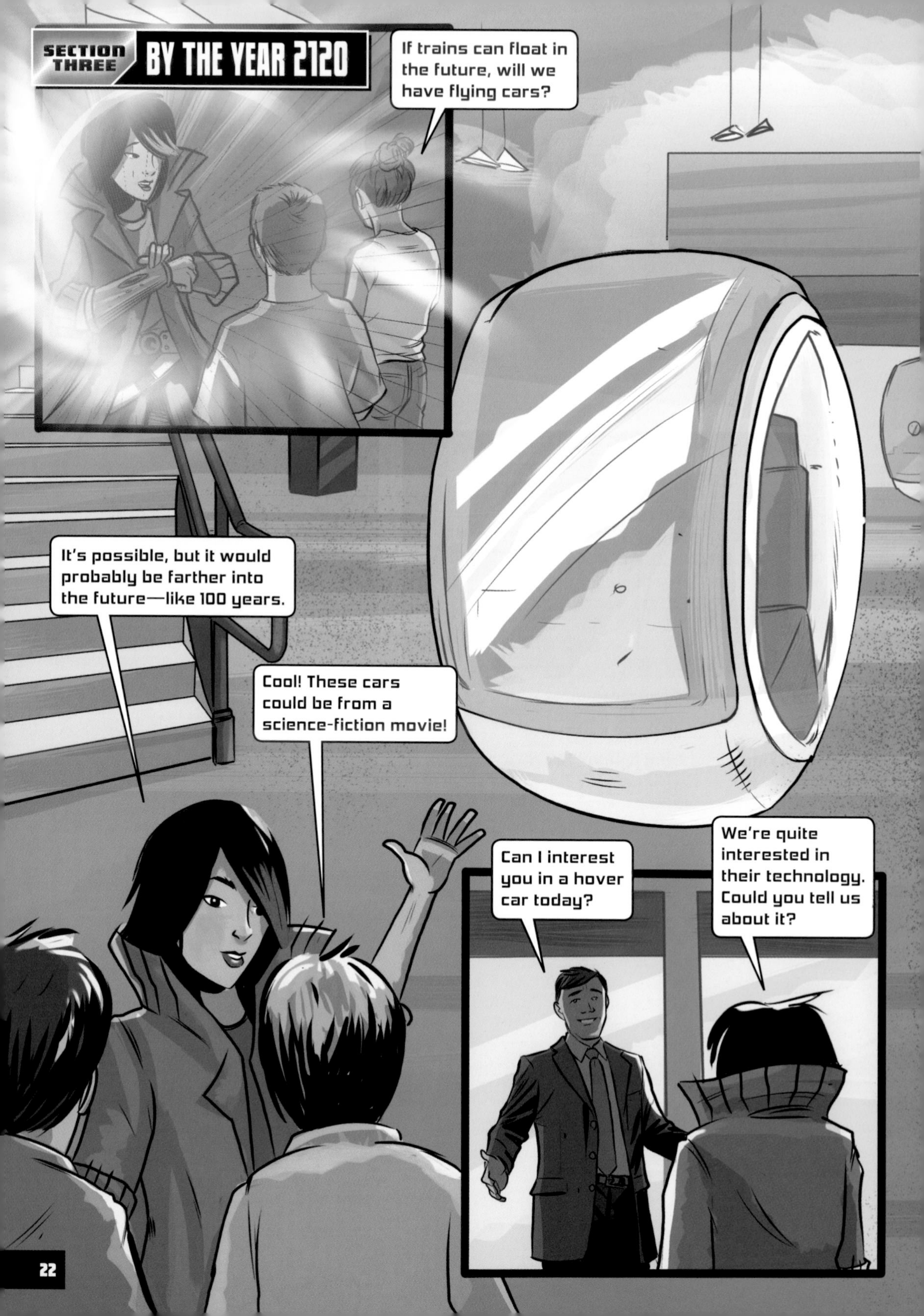

SECTION THREE
BY THE YEAR 2120
If trains can float in the future, will we have flying cars?
It's possible, but it would probably be farther into the future—like 100 years.
Cool! These cars could be from a science-fiction movie!
Can I interest you in a hover car today?
We're quite interested in their technology. Could you tell us about it?

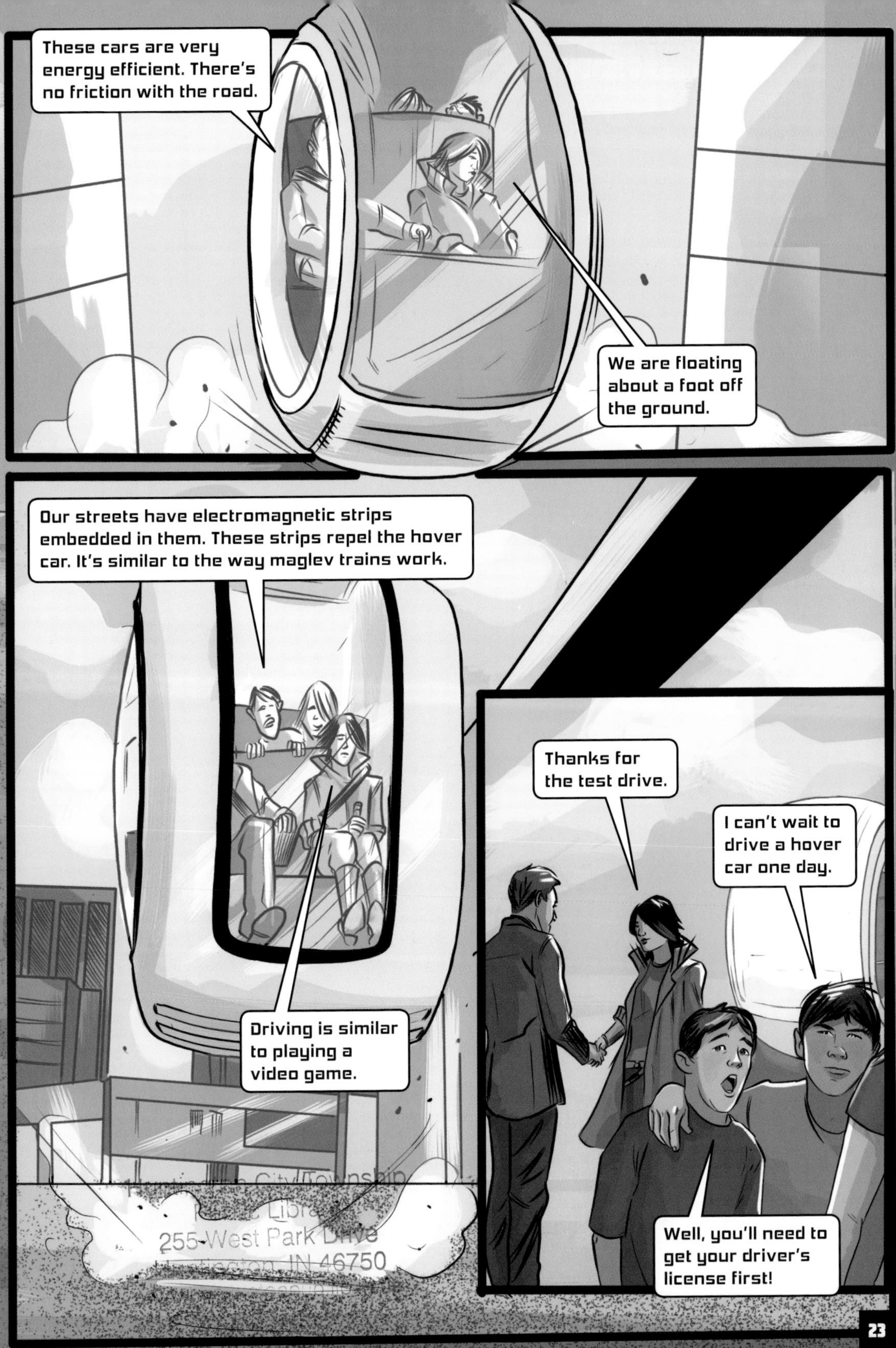
These cars are very energy efficient. There's no friction with the road.
We are floating about a foot off the ground.
Our streets have electromagnetic strips embedded in them. These strips repel the hover car. It's similar to the way maglev trains work.
Driving is similar to playing a video game.
Thanks for the test drive.
I can't wait to drive a hover car one day.
Well, you'll need to get your driver's license first!

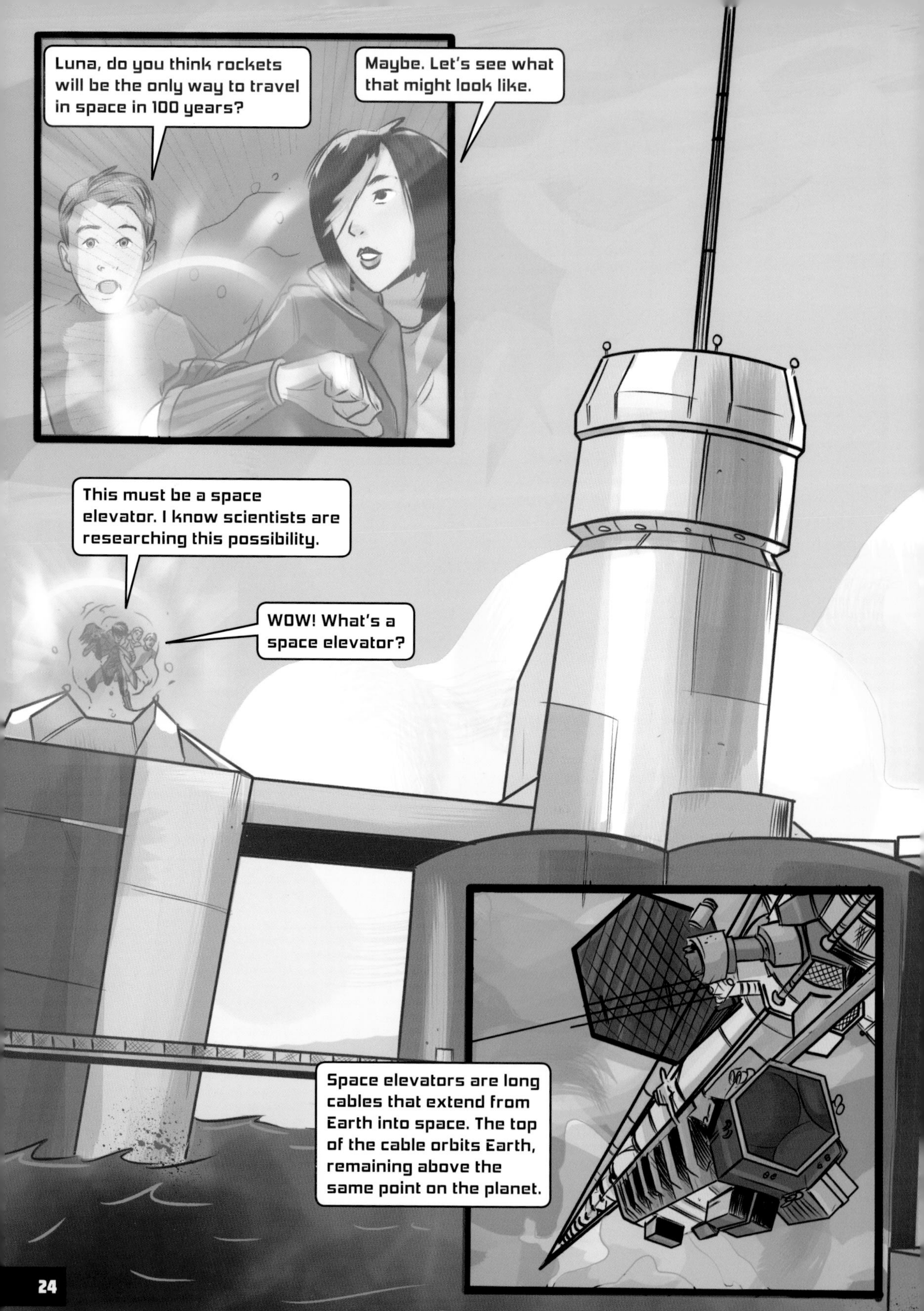
Luna, do you think rockets will be the only way to travel in space in 100 years?
Maybe. Let's see what that might look like.
This must be a space elevator. I know scientists are researching this possibility.
WOW! What's a space elevator?
Space elevators are long cables that extend from Earth into space. The top of the cable orbits Earth, remaining above the same point on the planet.

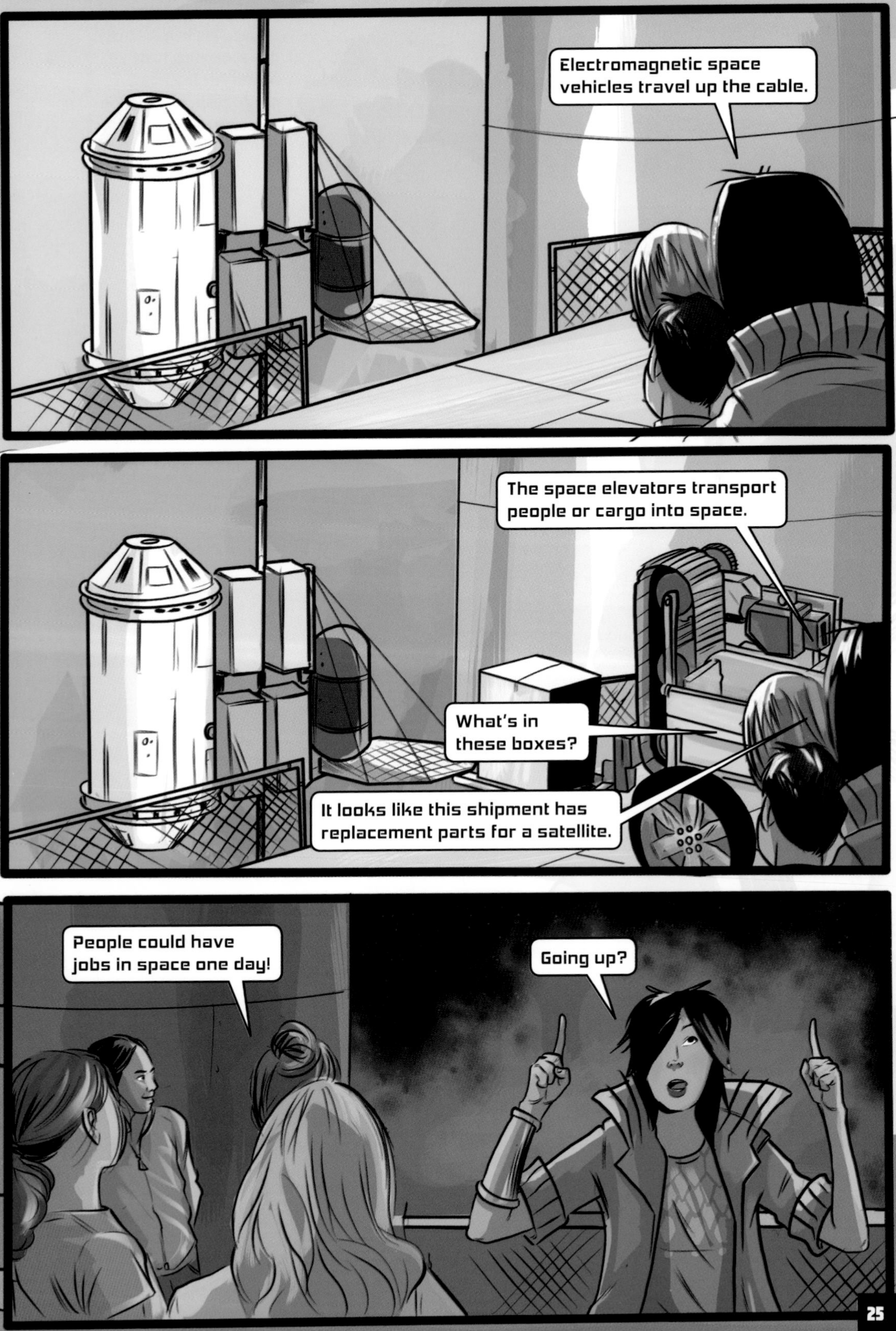
Electromagnetic space vehicles travel up the cable.
The space elevators transport people or cargo into space.
What's in these boxes?
It looks like this shipment has replacement parts for a satellite.
People could have jobs in space one day!
Going up?

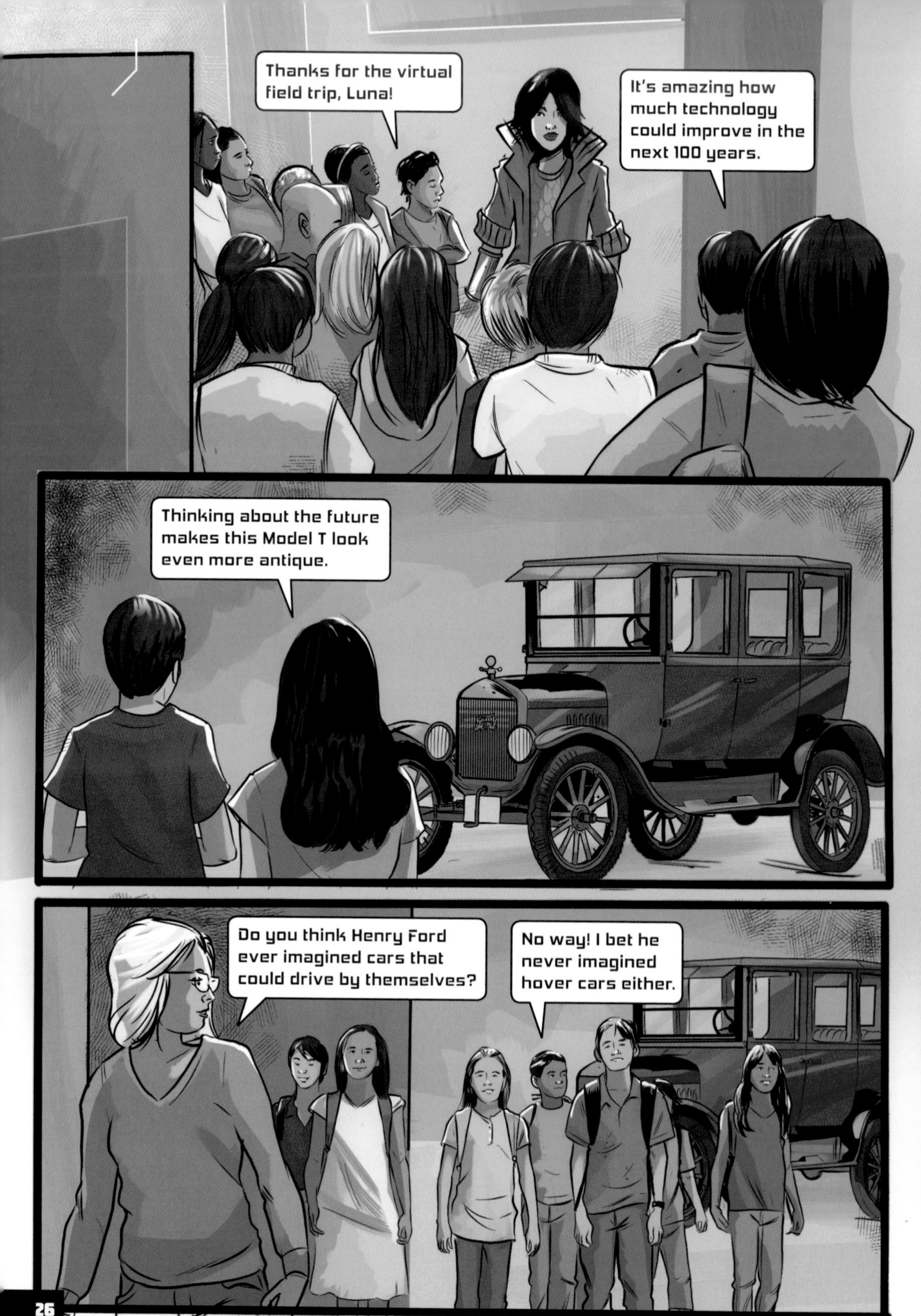
Thanks for the virtual field trip, Luna!
It's amazing how much technology could improve in the next 100 years.
Thinking about the future makes this Model T look even more antique.
Do you think Henry Ford ever imagined cars that could drive by themselves?
No way! I bet he never imagined hover cars either.

TELEPORTATION ||||||||||||||||||

Today some scientists are looking into the possibility of teleportation that instantly transports an object from one place to another. Teleporting people is far beyond the abilities of today's scientists, but it could be possible in the distant future. In 2014 scientists in the Netherlands teleported subatomic particles from one point to another, 3.3 yards (3 meters) apart. Perhaps hundreds of years from now, scientists will figure out how to teleport goods or even people

TRANSPORTATION

Orville and Wilbur Wright's first powered airplane flight lasted only 12 seconds. It flew at Kitty Hawk, North Carolina, on December 17, 1903. The flight distance was 120 feet (36 m).

James Watt designed the steam engine in 1769 in Scotland. In 1825 George Stephenson designed the world's first railway locomotive in England for Stockton and Darlington Railroad.

The Clermont was the first successful steamboat, built by Robert Fulton in 1807. Most steamboats built in the 1800s and 1900s had paddle wheels.

Colonel John Stevens is considered to be the father of American railroads. In 1826 he built a circular railroad track on his property in New Jersey.

Hydrogen may be a commonly used fuel for future transportation. The United States currently has 13 hydrogen filling stations. Eleven are in California, one in Connecticut, and one in South Carolina.

The Federal Aviation Administration (FAA) has given Amazon permission to research and test drone delivery in the United States. Amazon is restricted to testing no higher than 400 feet (122 m) and no faster than 100 miles (161 km) per hour. The drones must remain within sight of the operator. Additionally, drones must fly over private property.

LiftPort, a company in the United States, is currently researching the possibility of building a space elevator on the Moon. It could be used to transport building materials, supplies, and people to a possible future colony on the Moon.

Alternative fuels are a growing trend in motor vehicles. Battery-operated vehicles such as the three-wheeled Arcimoto SRK may be the way of the future. The Arcimoto can travel up to 130 miles (209 km) on a single charge of its battery pack.

LUNA LI

Futurists are scientists who systematically study and explore possibilities about the future of human society and life on Earth. Luna proved herself to be brilliant in this field at a young age. She excelled in STEM subjects and earned her PhD in Alternative Futures from the University of Hawaii at Manoa. Luna invented a gadget she calls the Future Scenario Generator (FSG) that she wears on her wrist. Luna inputs current and predicted data into the FSG. It then crunches the numbers and creates a portal to a holographic reality that humans can enter and interact with.

electromagnet (i-lek-troh-MAG-nuht)—a temporary magnet created when an electric current flows through a conductor

evolve (i-VAHLV)—when something develops over a long time with gradual changes

fossil fuels (FAH-suhl FYOOLZ)—natural fuels formed from the remains of plants and animals; coal, oil, and natural gas are fossil fuels

friction (FRIK-shuhn)—a force created when two objects rub together; friction slows down objects

hypersonic (hye-pur-SON-ik)—speed faster than Mach 5.0

laser (LAY-zur)—a narrow, intense beam of light

orbit (OR-bit)—the path of one body around another

radar (RAY-dar)—a device that uses radio waves to track the location of objects

replica (REP-luh-kuh)—an exact copy of something

subatomic (suhb-uh-TAH-mik)—describes things that are smaller than and part of an atom

suborbital flight (SUB-or-bit-ahl FLITE)—a flight into space that is too slow to orbit Earth

supersonic (soo-pur-SON-ik)—faster than the speed of sound

Dittmer, Lori. *The Future of Transportation.* Mankato, Minn.: Creative Education, 2013.

Parker, Steven. *Future Transport — By Air.* New York: Benchmark Books, 2011.

Parker, Steven. *Future Transport — On Land.* New York: Benchmark Books, 2011.

Schutten, Jan Paul. *Hello From 2030: the Science of the Future and You.* New York: Aladdin; Hillsboro, Oregon: Beyond Words, 2014.

INTERNET SITES

FactHound offers a safe, fun way to find Internet sites related to this book. All sites on FactHound have been researched by our staff.

Here's all you do:

Visit *www.facthound.com*

Type in this code: 9781491482667

Super-cool stuff! Check out projects, games and lots more at **www.capstonekids.com**